'There were two women in Zhenbao's life: one he called his white rose, the other his red rose. One was a spotless wife, the other a passionate mistress'

EILEEN CHANG

Born Zhang Ying, 30 September 1920, Shanghai
Died Eileen Chang, 8 September 1995, Westwood, California

This translation was first published by the *New York Review* in the USA, 2007. It was first published in Penguin Modern Classics the same year.

ALSO PUBLISHED BY PENGUIN BOOKS

Lust, Caution · *Love in a Fallen City*

EILEEN CHANG

Red Rose, White Rose

TRANSLATED BY KAREN S. KINGSBURY

PENGUIN BOOKS

PENGUIN CLASSICS

Published by the Penguin Group
Penguin Books Ltd, 80 Strand, London WC2R 0RL, England
Penguin Group (USA) Inc., 375 Hudson Street, New York, New York 10014, USA
Penguin Group (Canada), 90 Eglinton Avenue East, Suite 700, Toronto, Ontario, Canada M4P 2Y3 (a division of Pearson Penguin Canada Inc.)
Penguin Ireland, 25 St Stephen's Green, Dublin 2, Ireland (a division of Penguin Books Ltd)
Penguin Group (Australia), 250 Camberwell Road, Camberwell, Victoria 3124, Australia (a division of Pearson Australia Group Pty Ltd)
Penguin Books India Pvt Ltd, 11 Community Centre, Panchsheel Park, New Delhi – 110 017, India
Penguin Group (NZ), 67 Apollo Drive, Rosedale, North Shore 0632, New Zealand (a division of Pearson New Zealand Ltd)
Penguin Books (South Africa) (Pty) Ltd, 24 Sturdee Avenue, Rosebank, Johannesburg 2196, South Africa
Penguin Books Ltd, Registered Offices: 80 Strand, London WC2R 0RL, England
www.penguin.com

This translation first published in *Love in a Fallen City* in Penguin Classics 2007
This edition published in Penguin Classics 2011
3

Typeset by Jouve (UK), Milton Keynes
Printed in England by Clays Ltd, St Ives plc

ISBN: 978-0-141-19614-5

Red Rose, White Rose

There were two women in Zhenbao's life: one he called his white rose, the other his red rose. One was a spotless wife, the other a passionate mistress. Isn't that just how the average man describes a chaste widow's devotion to her husband's memory – as spotless, and passionate too?

Maybe every man has had two such women – at least two. Marry a red rose and eventually she'll be a mosquito-blood streak smeared on the wall, while the white one is 'moonlight in front of my bed.' Marry a white rose, and before long she'll be a grain of sticky rice that's gotten stuck to your clothes; the red one, by then, is a scarlet beauty mark just over your heart.

But Zhenbao wasn't like that; he was logical and thorough. He was, in this respect, the ideal modern Chinese man. If he did bump into something that was less than ideal, he bounced it around in his mind for a while and – poof! – it was idealized: then everything fell into place.

Zhenbao had launched his career the proper way, by going to the West to get his degree and factory training. He was smart and well educated, and having worked his way through school, he had the energy and determination of a self-made man. Now he held an upper-level position in a well-known foreign textile company. His wife was a university graduate, and she came from a good family. She was gentle and pretty, and she'd never been a party girl. One daughter, age nine: already they'd made plans for her college tuition.

Never had a son been more filial, more considerate, than Zhenbao was to his mother; never was a brother more thoughtful or helpful to his siblings. At work he was the most hard-working and devoted of colleagues; to his friends, the kindest, truest, and most generous of men. Zhenbao's life was a complete success. If he had believed in reincarnation – he didn't – he'd have hoped simply to pick up a new name, then come back and live the same life all over again.

Rich idlers laughed at Zhenbao and called him vulgar – literary youths and progressive types did too. But since he was vulgar in a Western way, they didn't really hold it against him. Zhenbao wasn't tall, but he was vigorous and quick. He had a soy-brown face and wore black-rimmed glasses, with something peculiarly unresolved in his facial expression. His posture was excellent and he didn't joke around – unless, that is, it was appropriate to joke. He seemed frank and open, a man you could take in at a glance – and if you couldn't quite pinpoint the sincerity in his eyes, those eyeglasses were proof enough.

Zhenbao came from a poor family. If he hadn't struggled to rise in the world, he probably would have had to stand behind a counter in a shop, and then his whole existence would have been one tiny round of ignorance and stupidity. Instead, starting in on his new job after his studies abroad, his window opened up on the whole world: he had plenty of opportunities to look forward to and the benefits of an unfettered mind. An amazing degree of freedom, all in all. And yet the average man's life, no matter how good, is only a 'peach blossom fan.' Like the loyal, beleaguered beauty in the story, you bang your head and blood drips on the fan. Add a few strokes of ink, and the bloodstain becomes a peach blossom. Zhenbao's fan was still blank, but he had a dry brush, a wet inkstone, a sunny window, and a clean table – all just waiting for him to lower his brush and begin.

That blank fan did have some hazy figures in the background, like the images of people in old-fashioned clothes that one sees printed in light purple ink on elegant, mock-antique stationery. Before the wife and mistress, there had been two insignificant women.

The first was a Paris whore.

Zhenbao had studied textile manufacturing at a school in Edinburgh. Poor students don't have a chance to see much when abroad, and all that Zhenbao remembered of Britain was the Underground, cabbage, fog, hunger, and stuffing himself sick. As for things like opera, not until he returned home to Shanghai did he have an opportunity to see a Russian company perform. But one summer he'd laid out some money, taken off some time, and gone on a tour of the Continent. When he got to Paris, naturally he wanted to see how very naughty the Parisians were, except that he didn't have any friends who knew the town well enough to show him around. He couldn't afford – and didn't want – that kind of friend. So he plunged in all on his own, afraid of what it might cost, afraid of being cheated too.

One evening in Paris, he found himself with nothing to do. He'd eaten supper early and was walking to his lodgings in a quiet back street. 'And all my friends will think that I've really seen Paris,' he said to himself, almost plaintively. The streetlamps had already been lit but overhead the sun still shone, dropping bit by bit down to the roofs of the square cement buildings, dropping farther and farther. The shimmering white of the roofs seemed to be crumbling away. Zhenbao walked down the street, feeling forlorn. In one of the houses someone was playing a piano with one hand, picking out the notes: Christmas songs played very slowly, one after another. Christmas carols are joyful on Christmas Eve, but this was a summer afternoon on a long quiet street flooded with sunlight. The timing felt all wrong, like a dream so mixed-up and meaningless that it was almost funny. Zhenbao didn't know why, but he couldn't bear the sound of that one-finger melody.

He picked up his pace; his hand started to sweat in his pocket. He walked quickly, but then the woman in front of him, wearing a black dress, slowed down; she turned her head just a bit and gave him a glance. She was wearing a red slip under her black-lace dress. Zhenbao liked red lingerie. He hadn't realized that a woman of this sort would be in this neighborhood, with a little hotel nearby.

Years later, when Zhenbao was telling the story to friends, he would adopt a mocking manner, happy but a tad rueful. 'Before I went to Paris,' he'd say, 'I was just a boy! I really ought to go back someday, for old times' sake.' The memory should have been a romantic one, but oddly enough he couldn't recall any of the romantic parts, only the upsetting ones. Foreigners always have more body odor than Chinese people do; this woman couldn't stop worrying about it. He noticed how she'd half consciously raise one arm and turn her head to sniff. The armpits of her clothing were sprayed with perfume; cheap perfume mixed with armpit odor and sour sweat made for a strange smell that he couldn't get out of his head. But what he hated most was her constant worrying. When she came out of the bathroom in her slip, she rested her hand high on the wall, tilted her head to the side, and smiled at him – but he knew that at some level she was sniffing herself.

With a woman like this – even with a woman like this! – though he could spend money on her, he couldn't be her master. The half hour he spent with her filled him with shame.

There was another detail he could never forget. She was putting her clothes back on, pulling her dress over her head, and when she was half there, with the fabric still piled up around her shoulders, she stopped for a moment as if she'd thought of something. Right then, he saw her in the mirror. She had a mass of tousled blonde hair, pulled tight by the dress so that only her long, thin face showed. Her eyes were blue, a blue that ran down into the shadows under her eyes, while the eyes themselves were like two transparent glass balls. It was a cold, severe, masculine face, the face of an ancient warrior. Zhenbao was badly shaken.

When he came out, the sun was still shining, with the shadows of the trees lying crooked in the sunlit street. This too was not right. It was terrifying.

Whoring can be sleazy, low-class, filthy-miserable, and it won't matter – that just makes it all the earthier. But it wasn't like that, not this time. Later, when Zhenbao had figured out how to get what he wanted out of a whore, he'd think back to that time in Paris, his first time, when he'd been such a fool. Now he was the master of his own world.

From that day on, Zhenbao was determined to create a world that was 'right,' and to carry it with him wherever he went. In that little pocket-size world of his, he was the absolute master.

Zhenbao lived in England for a considerable time. His factory internship paid a stipend, and he rustled up odd jobs on the side. Once he'd made himself a bit more comfortable, financially speaking, he acquired a few girlfriends. He was a nice fellow, and he wanted to meet a nice girl, not some prostitute. But he was also a busy man who couldn't spend lots of time on courting; naturally he liked girls who were a little more forthright. There were only a few Chinese girls in Edinburgh, two of them classmates who hailed from the inland provinces – he found them too affected, too churchy, altogether too pious. Nowadays the churches have become something of a social scene, with quite a few beauties on display, but ten years ago, the fervent churchgoers who had love in their hearts weren't, in fact, lovely. The lively ones were the overseas Chinese; mixed-blood girls went even farther.

Zhenbao met a girl named Rose. She was his first love, which is why he also likened his two later women to roses. Rose's father was a good-looking English businessman who'd lived in southern China for many years and then, thanks to a passing fancy, married a Cantonese girl and brought her home to Edinburgh. The wife had to be living in the house still, but she was practically invisible and never took part in social events. Rose attended an English school, and because she wasn't completely English she acted more English than the English themselves. The English students liked to affect a certain dashing indifference, and when something really important was at stake, the affectation grew even stronger. Zhenbao couldn't figure out whether or not Rose really loved him; he, for his part, was rather dazzled. They both liked to do things fast, and on Saturday nights they made the rounds of different dance halls. When they weren't out on the dance floor, but just sitting around and talking, Rose never seemed to pay much attention. She'd take out some matches and try to balance a glass on top of them. Zhenbao was supposed to help. That was Rose: solemn as could be when she was horsing around. There was a canary at her place, and whenever it sang she thought it was calling to her. 'Yes, bird?' she'd answer right off, standing on tiptoe with her hands behind her back, and her face tilted up toward the birdcage. Her tan face was long, not round like a child's, but at such moments she seemed remarkably childlike. She'd gaze wide-eyed at the bird in the cage, the whites of her eyes tinged blue, as if she were staring into deep blue skies.

Rose may have been the most ordinary of girls, but her very youth made her remarkably hard to read. Like that canary – calling out but not really saying anything to anyone.

Her short skirt ended above her knees, and her legs were light and nimble, as delicately made as wooden legs in a shop window; her skin was as smooth and glistening as freshly planed and oiled wood. Her hair was cut very short, shaved down to a little point at the nape of her neck. No hair to protect her neck, no sleeves to protect her arms – Rose did not watch her words, and her body was open for the taking. She was carefree with Zhenbao, and he put that down to her being innocent, but her being so carefree with everyone struck him as slightly nutty. This kind of woman was common enough in foreign countries, but in China it would never do. Marrying her, then transplanting her to his hometown – that would be a big waste of time and money, not a good deal at all.

One evening he drove her home, as he often did. But this time it seemed different because he was going to leave England soon and if he had anything to say he should have said it by now. He hadn't. Her house was quite far from town. The faint black-and-white of the late-night road patted their faces like a powder puff. The conversation in the car was desultory in the English fashion, starting and stopping again. Rose knew that she had already lost him. Then, out of a kind of hopeless obstinacy, her heart caught fire. 'Stop here,' she said, when they had almost reached her house. 'I don't want to let my family see us saying good-bye.' 'I'd kiss you even in front of them,' Zhenbao said, smiling. He reached out to wrap his arm around her shoulder, and she buried her face into his chest. The car kept going – they were well past her house before it stopped. Zhenbao slid his hand under her velvet coat and pulled her toward him. Behind her aching-cold diamonds, crinkly silver lace, hundreds of exquisite nuisances, her young body seemed to leap out of her clothes. Zhenbao kissed her, and tears streamed over her face till neither of them could tell who was crying. Outside the car, a damp, limitless fog floated in the wind. Its emptiness sapped their strength, and all they could do was hang on to each other. Rose clung to his neck, this way then that, trying to pull ever closer, wishing she could fuse her body with his, press herself into it. Zhenbao was so confused that he couldn't think. He had never dreamed that Rose loved him so much; he could have done whatever he wanted. But . . . this would not do. Rose, after all, was a decent girl. This sort of thing was not for him.

Rose's body leapt out of her clothes, leapt onto his body, but he was his own master.

Afterward, even he was surprised by his self-control. He'd hardened his heart and taken Rose home. Just before he left, he held her moist face, with its sniffles and tears and quivering eyelashes that fluttered in his palms like some tiny winged creature. In later days, he'd recall this experience whenever he needed to rally his strength: 'If you could control yourself then, in that situation, surely you can do so now.'

His behavior that evening filled him with astonishment and admiration, and yet in his heart he felt regret. Without admitting it, he felt quite a lot of regret.

He seldom mentioned the incident, but there was not one of his friends who was unaware of Zhenbao's reputation as a regular Liu Xiahui, a man who could keep perfectly calm with a beautiful woman in his lap. Word had gotten around.

Zhenbao's grades were excellent, and before he'd even graduated he was offered a position at Great

Beneficence, an English dyeing and weaving company; he started there immediately upon his return to Shanghai. Zhenbao's family home was in Jiangwan, quite far from his job, and at first he stayed with some old family friends. But when his younger brother, Tong Dubao, finished his secondary schooling, Zhenbao made arrangements for Dubao to come and live with him, so he could help him with his studies; he wanted Dubao to take the entrance exam for the technical school that was affiliated with the Great Beneficence Dyeing and Weaving Company. They couldn't both stay in the friends' home; that would be too great an imposition. As it happened, an old classmate of Zhenbao's, Wang Shihong, had an empty room in his place. Wang Shihong had been abroad and had come back to Shanghai two years before Zhenbao; now he was living in an apartment on Ferguson Road. He and Zhenbao struck a deal – the room was even furnished.

On the day he was to move in, Zhenbao left work just after dusk. He and his brother were busy supervising the coolies as they carried the trunks in, and Wang Shihong was standing arms akimbo in the doorway, when a woman walked in from the room behind. She was washing her hair, which was all lathered up with shampoo, the white curls standing high on her head like a marble sculpture. 'While the workmen are here,' she said to Shihong, holding her hair with her hands, 'have them arrange all the furniture and things. It's no use asking our majordomo to help: he'll just make excuses – if he's not in the mood he won't do anything.'

'Let me introduce everyone,' said Wang Shihong. 'Zhenbao, Dubao, my wife. I believe you haven't met yet?'

The woman withdrew her hand from her hair to shake hands with the guests, but seeing the shampoo on her fingers, she hesitated. She nodded and smiled instead, then wiped her fingers on her dressing gown. A little shampoo splashed the back of Zhenbao's hand. Instead of rubbing it off, he let it dry there. The skin puckered up slightly, as if a mouth were lightly sucking at the spot.

Mrs Wang turned and went back into the other room. Zhenbao directed the workers as they moved the bed and wardrobe, but he felt troubled, and the sucking sensation was still there. His mind wandered as he headed to the bathroom to wash his hands, thinking about this Mrs Wang. He'd heard that she was an overseas Chinese from Singapore who, when she was studying in London, was quite a party girl. She and Wang Shihong got married in London, but Zhenbao had been too busy to attend the wedding. Seeing her was much better than hearing about her: under her white, shampoo-sculpted hair was a tawny-gold face, the skin glistening and the flesh so firm that her eyes rose at a long upward slant, like the eyes of an actress. Her striped dressing gown, worn without a belt, hugged her body loosely, and the black-and-white stripes hinted at her figure, each line, each inch, fully alive. People like to say that the wide, long-sleeved gowns of former times didn't flatter curvaceous beauties, but Zhenbao had just discovered that this was not the case. He turned on the faucet. The water wasn't very hot, though the water heater downstairs was certainly on, and yet the lukewarm stream seemed to have a lighted wick running through it. Twisting and winding, the water ran from the faucet, every inch of it alive, while Zhenbao's mind went running off to who knows where.

Wang Shihong heard the sound of running water and came into the bathroom. 'Do you want to take a bath? The water never comes up hot in this bathroom. The hot water pipe wasn't connected properly. That's one bad thing about this apartment. If you want to wash, come into our bathroom.'

'Oh no, please don't bother,' Zhenbao said. 'Isn't your wife washing her hair?'

'She must be finished by now. I'll go and have a look.'

'Oh, really, it's not that important.'

Wang Shihong went to speak with his wife, and his wife said, 'I'm just finishing. Tell the amah to draw him a bath.'

A little later, Wang Shihong told Zhenbao to bring his soap, towel, and clothes into their bathroom. Mrs Wang was still in front of the mirror, struggling to get a comb through her tightly permed hair. The bathroom was full of steam, and the night wind blew in through the open window. On the floor, clusters of fallen hair swirled about like ghostly figures.

Zhenbao stood outside the door holding his towel and watching the tangled hair, in the glare of the bathroom light, drifting across the floor. He felt quite agitated. He liked women who were fiery and impetuous, the kind you couldn't marry. Here was one who was already a wife, and a friend's wife at that, so there couldn't be any danger, but . . . look at that hair! It was everywhere. She was everywhere, tugging and pulling at him.

The couple stood in the bathroom talking, but the water filling the tub was loud and Zhenbao couldn't hear what they said. When the tub was full, they came out so he could take his bath. After his bath, Zhenbao crouched down and started picking up stray hairs from the floor tiles and twisting them together. The permed hair had turned yellow at the ends; it was stiff, like fine electrical wire. He stuffed it into his pocket. His hand stayed there, and his whole body tingled. But this was too ridiculous. He extracted the hair from his pocket and tossed it into the spittoon.

Carrying his soap and towel, he returned to his own room – Dubao was opening the trunks and arranging things. 'What kind of person could the previous tenant have been?' Dubao asked. 'Look, here under the chair slipcovers, and under the carpet here – those have got to be cigarette burns! And these marks under the table – they won't come off. Mr Wang isn't going to blame us is he?'

'Of course not. They must know about it already. Besides, we're classmates from way back, so they won't be as petty as you are!' Zhenbao smiled.

Dubao fell silent. Then he asked, 'Do you know who the previous tenant was?'

'His family name is Sun I think; he's back from England, teaching at a university now. Why do you ask?'

Dubao smiled before he spoke. 'Just now when you were gone, the majordomo and the amah came to put up the curtains. They said something about not knowing how long we'll stay, and they said that Mr Wang had wanted to kick out the man who lived here before. Mr Wang was planning to go to Singapore on business, and he should have left a long time ago, but something happened and he got nervous – he wouldn't leave till the other fellow was out. Neither of them budged – not for two whole months.'

Zhenbao told him to shush. 'How can you believe such nonsense! When you live in someone's house, the first rule is never to discuss the family with the servants. That only leads to trouble!' Dubao didn't say anything more.

A bit later, the amah came to call them to dinner, and the brothers went into the dining room together. The cooking in the Wang household had a slightly Southeast Asian flavor, Chinese food prepared Western style, and the main dish was lamb curry. Mrs Wang had nothing but a thin slice of toast and a piece of ham in front of her. She even cut the fatty part off the meat and gave it to her husband.

'Such a small appetite?' Zhenbao smiled.

'She's afraid of getting fat,' said Shihong.

Zhenbao's face expressed disbelief. 'Mrs Wang looks just right. She's not fat at all.'

'I've just lost five pounds, so I'm a lot thinner than I was,' she said.

Shihong grinned and reached over to pinch her cheek. 'A lot thinner? Then what's this?'

His wife gave him a sharp glance. 'That's the London lamb I ate last year.' Everyone laughed hard at this.

Even though the Tong brothers and Mrs Wang had just met for the first time, their hostess hadn't bothered to change before coming to the dinner table. She was still in her dressing gown and her hair was still wet. A white towel was wrapped carelessly around it, and every so often the towel dripped, spangling her eyebrows. Dubao was a country boy, and Mrs Wang's free-and-easy ways struck him as strange indeed. But even Zhenbao found her pretty remarkable. Mrs Wang was extremely attentive, asking all sorts of questions. She wasn't very good at keeping house, that was clear, but she did know how to entertain.

'I haven't had time to tell you,' Shihong said to Zhenbao, 'but I'm leaving tomorrow. I have some business in Singapore. It's good that you've moved in and can take care of things here.'

'Mrs Wang is very capable,' Zhenbao said with a smile. 'She'll be taking care of us, I'm sure. I very much doubt that it will be us taking care of her.'

'Don't be fooled by her chatter,' said Shihong. 'She doesn't understand a thing. She's been in China for three years now, but she still isn't used to it here, and she can't really speak Chinese well.'

Mrs Wang smiled slightly and didn't disagree. She merely summoned the amah to fetch a bottle of medicine from the cabinet, and poured out a spoonful.

Zhenbao saw the thick liquid, like white paint, in the spoon, and winced. 'Is that cream of calcium? I've taken that before – it tastes terrible.'

Mrs Wang emptied the spoon down her throat. For a moment she was speechless, but then she swallowed the medicine. 'It's like drinking a wall!' she said. Zhenbao smiled again. 'When Mrs Wang talks, she hits the nail right on the head!'

'Mr Tong,' said Mrs Wang, 'don't keep calling me Mrs Wang.' She got up and went over to a desk near the window. It's true, Zhenbao was thinking to himself, the name 'Mrs Wang' is just too commonplace. She sat at the desk, apparently writing something. Shihong went over to her, put his hand on her shoulder, and bent down to ask, 'You're perfectly healthy, so why are you taking doses of that?'

Mrs Wang kept on writing, without turning her head. 'The heat is rising in my system – I've got a pimple on my face.'

'Where?' said Shihong, leaning his face close. She moved aside lightly, frowning and smiling at once. 'Hey there, hey there!' she warned him.

Dubao, raised in an old-fashioned family, had never seen a husband and wife like this. He was unable to sit still and left to admire the scenery. He opened the glass door and walked onto the balcony. Zhenbao went on peeling an apple with a fair degree of composure. But Mrs Wang came back across the room, and thrust a piece of paper at him. 'There, I too have a given name,' she said.

'The way you write Chinese characters, you shouldn't show them around,' Shihong said with a smile. 'People will just laugh.'

When Zhenbao saw the three crooked words on the paper, each one bigger than the last, and the last one breaking apart into three distinct fragments – wang jiAO ʀUI – he really had to laugh.

'I told you people would laugh, didn't I?' Shihong said with a clap of his hands.

'No, no,' said Zhenbao, controlling himself. 'Really it's a pretty name!'

'Those overseas Chinese – the names they pick never have any style,' said Shihong.

Pouting, Jiaorui grabbed the piece of paper and crumpled it up. She turned on her heels and walked off, seemingly in a huff. Not thirty seconds later she came back with an open jar of candied walnuts, which she'd already started to eat, and she offered them to Zhenbao and Dubao.

'I thought you were afraid of getting fat!' laughed Shihong.

'It's true,' said Zhenbao. 'Sweets are very fattening.'

'You don't know about those overseas Chinese,

they –' Shihong started to say, but Jiaorui hit him. 'It's always "they, them, those overseas Chinese"!' she said. 'Don't call me "them"!'

Shihong went right on. 'They have the bad habits of the Chinese and the bad habits of foreigners as well. From the foreigners they learn to be afraid of getting fat, won't eat this, won't eat that, always taking purgatives but can't stop eating sweets. But then – go ahead, just ask her! If you ask her why she's eating this, she'll say she's had a little cough recently, and candied walnuts are good for a cough.'

'That really is the old Chinese way,' Zhenbao said with a smile. 'Anything you like to eat is, of course, good for something.'

Jiaorui picked up a walnut and slid it between her teeth. She pointed her little finger at Zhenbao. 'Stop that now – there really is some truth to it!'

To Zhenbao, she seemed drunk. Fearing the kind of faux pas that so often follows drink, he mumbled something inconsequential and strolled onto the balcony. The breeze was cool on his skin: most likely his face had been pretty red a moment before. Now he was even more troubled. He'd just put an end to his relationship with Rose, and here she was again, in a new body, with a new soul – and another man's wife. But this woman went even further than Rose. When she was in the room, the walls seemed to be covered with figures in red chalk, pictures of her half naked, on the left, on the right, everywhere. Why did he keep running into this kind of woman? Was it his fault that he always reacted the way he did? Surely that couldn't be. After all, there really weren't many women of this sort, not among the pure Chinese. He'd just returned to China, so he was running with the half-Chinese, half-Western crowd. Any Chinese he met while abroad was 'an old friend found in a faraway land.' When he returned home and saw those 'old friends' again, the first time they met they were bosom friends, the second time mere acquaintances, and by the third time they were strangers to each other.

And yet, when it came to this Wang Jiaorui, hadn't Shihong done pretty well for himself by marrying her? Of course, Wang Shihong's father had money; if a man had to forge ahead on his own, as Zhenbao did, such a woman would be a major impediment. And he wasn't easygoing like Wang Shihong, who let a woman flout every rule. What was the point if you had to argue all day long? That was sure to sap a man's energy and drain him of ambition. Of course . . . she was like this precisely because her husband couldn't control her; if Wang Shihong had managed to get a handle on her, she wouldn't be quite so unruly.

Zhenbao leaned on the railing, his arms folded. Down below, an electric tram with a brightly burning lamp stopped at the entrance of the building. Several people got on and off, and the lamp moved away. Wide and quiet, the street stretched beyond him; the only light was from a little restaurant on the first floor. Two leaves skittered by in the wind like ragged shoes not worn by anyone, just walking along by themselves. So many people in the world – but they won't be coming home with you. When night fell and silence took over – or when, as could happen at any time, you stood at the brink of death – there in the dark, you needed a wife you really loved, otherwise there would be nothing but loneliness. Zhenbao didn't think this through clearly, but he was overwhelmed by a sense of foreboding.

Shihong and his wife were chatting as they walked onto the balcony. 'Is your hair dry?' Shihong asked. 'If you stand in the breeze your cough is going to get worse.'

'It doesn't matter,' said Jiaorui, unwrapping the towel and shaking out her hair.

Zhenbao figured that since Shihong was leaving the next day, the couple would want to speak in privacy. Raising a hand to disguise a forced yawn, he said, 'We'll go to bed now. Dubao has to get up very early tomorrow so he can go to school and get a student handbook.'

'I'm leaving in the afternoon,' Shihong said, 'so I probably won't see you.' The two men shook hands and said good-bye. Zhenbao and Dubao went to their room.

The next day, when Zhenbao came back from work and pressed the doorbell, Jiaorui opened the door, phone receiver in hand. It was dim in the hallway, which made it hard to see, but Shihong's hat and coat were gone from the coatrack, along with the leather suitcase that had been under the rack. He must have left already. Taking off his coat and hanging it on the rack, Zhenbao heard Jiaorui dial a phone number in the other room. 'Please ask Mr Sun to come to the phone,' she said. Zhenbao listened. He heard her ask, 'Is this Timmy? No, I'm not going out today, I'm at home waiting for a boyfriend.' She started to giggle. 'Who is he? I'm not telling you. Why should I tell you? . . . Ah, so you're not interested? Not even interested in yourself, are you . . . Anyway, I'm waiting for him to come for tea at five o'clock. I'm waiting specially for him, so don't come over.'

Zhenbao went to his room without waiting for her to finish. His brother wasn't there, or in the bathroom either. He went out to see if he was on the balcony, and Jiaorui emerged from the living room to greet him. 'Dubao asked me to tell you that he's making the rounds of the used bookstores to see if he can find some books.'

'Oh, thank you,' said Zhenbao. He took a good long look. She was wearing a long dress that trailed on the floor, a dress of such intense, fresh, and wet green that anything it touched turned the same color. When she moved a little, the air was streaked with green. The dress had been cut a bit too small, it seemed: the seams along the side were split open an inch and a half, then laced together, in a crisscross pattern, over a green satin strip that didn't fully cover a startling pink slip. Looked at too long, those eye-popping colors would prove blinding. Only Jiaorui could wear a dress like that with such utter insouciance.

'Would you like some tea?' she asked, turning back into the living room. She sat down at the table, and lifted the pot to pour the tea. The table was set for two, with a plate of butter biscuits and toast. Zhenbao stood by the glass door.

'Isn't there a guest coming?'

'We won't wait for him. Let's go ahead and have something to eat.'

Zhenbao hesitated, unable to figure out what she had in mind. Then, just for the time being, he sat down.

'Do you take milk?' Jiaorui asked.

'Either way.'

'Oh, that's right, you like green tea. You were abroad so many years and couldn't get it there – that's what you said yesterday.'

'You have a good memory.'

Getting up to ring the bell, Jiaorui threw him a glance. 'No, you don't know. Usually my memory is terrible.'

Zhenbao's heart jumped, and he was knocked off balance. The amah came in. 'Make two cups of green tea,' Jiaorui ordered.

'Ask her to bring another teacup and plate while she's at it,' said Zhenbao, 'for the guest who's coming later.'

Jiaorui gave him a sharp look. 'Who is this guest that you're so anxious about? Amah, bring me a pen and a piece of paper.' She dashed off a note, then pushed it across to Zhenbao. Two lines, simple and succinct: *Dear Timmy, So very sorry, but I have something to do today. I've gone out. – Jiaorui*. She folded the paper over and gave it to the amah. 'Mr Sun will come in a little while. When he does, give this to him and tell him I'm not home.'

The amah went out. Zhenbao took a biscuit. 'I don't understand you,' he said. 'Why go to so much trouble, asking a man to come to your house, then turn him away empty-handed?'

Jiaorui leaned forward, carefully considering the selection of biscuits on the plate, but she couldn't find any that she liked. 'When I asked him to come I didn't plan to turn him away.'

'Oh? A last-minute decision?'

'Don't you know the saying? It's a woman's prerogative to change her mind.'

The amah brought the green tea, leaves floating all over the surface of the water. Zhenbao held the glass in both hands without drinking. His eyes were fixed on the tea but his mind was elsewhere, working things out. Jiaorui was still carrying on with that Mr Sun behind her husband's back, and evidently she was worried that Zhenbao would see what was going on. That's why she'd put on this sweet act today. She wanted to win him over so he'd keep his mouth shut. But in fact Zhenbao had no intention of interfering in their private lives. It wasn't that his bond with Wang Shihong was too weak – even if they'd been blood brothers, stirring up disputes between a husband and wife was not his style. Even so, this woman could cause a lot of trouble. Zhenbao redoubled his caution.

Jiaorui set down her tea glass and rose to get a jar of peanut butter from the cabinet. 'I'm a trashy person, and I like to eat trashy things.'

'Oh, my! This stuff is very rich, very fattening!'

Jiaorui took off the lid. 'I love breaking the rules. Don't you approve of rule-breaking?'

Zhenbao put his hand on top of the glass jar. 'No.'

Jiaorui hesitated for a long moment. Then she said, 'How about this? You put some on the bread for me. I'm sure you won't give me too much.'

Her expression was so pitiful that he couldn't help laughing. Zhenbao spread peanut butter on the bread. Jiaorui watched him closely over the edge of her cup, pursed her lips, and laughed. 'Do you know why I had you do it for me? If I did it myself, all of a sudden I might turn conscientious and spread it as thin as possible. But I know that you'd feel bad if you only gave me a little!' At this they both laughed. Unable to resist Jiaorui's childlike charm, Zhenbao gradually softened.

As they were drinking their tea, the doorbell sounded. Zhenbao got restless. For the third time now he asked, 'Is that the guest you invited? Don't you feel embarrassed?' Jiaorui shrugged.

Taking his glass with him, Zhenbao went out to the balcony. 'When he comes back through the door, I want to see the kind of person he is.'

'Him?' said Jiaorui, following behind. 'Very pretty. Too, too pretty.'

'You don't like pretty men?' said Zhenbao, leaning against the railing.

'Men should not be pretty. Men get spoiled even more easily than women do.'

Zhenbao lowered his eyelids, then looked at her. 'You shouldn't talk about others,' he said with a smile. 'You've been terribly spoiled.'

'Maybe. But you're just the opposite. You deny yourself when in fact you like to eat and play around as much as I do.'

'Really?' Zhenbao laughed. 'And you know all about it!'

Jiaorui looked down and started picking tea leaves out of her glass. She kept picking away, until at last she took a sip. Zhenbao too drank his tea in silence.

A little while later, a man in a Western suit came out of the building. Zhenbao couldn't see much from the third floor, but it looked like the man rushed around the corner, his body tense with anger.

'Poor guy,' Zhenbao couldn't help saying. 'He came all this way for nothing!'

'So what? He has nothing to do all day long! I too have nothing to do, but I have no respect for people like me. What I like most is to wrest a bit of time from a man who's already very busy – the way a tiger seizes its prey. Pretty despicable, don't you think?'

Zhenbao was leaning against the railing. He tapped his foot against the railing and then, bit by bit, not entirely intentionally, he started kicking at her rattan chair. When the chair shook, the flesh on her arm trembled slightly. She wasn't fat at all, but because of her small frame she seemed plump. 'So you like busy men?' Zhenbao smiled.

Jiaorui hid her eyes with her hand. 'Actually, it doesn't matter. My heart's an apartment.'

'So – is there an empty room for rent?' Jiaorui didn't answer. 'I'm not used to living in an apartment. I want to live in a single-family house.'

She gave a little grunt of disbelief. 'Well,' she said, 'Let's see if you can tear one down and build the other!'

Zhenbao gave her chair a good hard kick. 'Just watch me!'

Jiaorui took her hand from her eyes and gave him a long look. 'You're wicked!'

'Can't help myself, with you.'

'Come on, be serious,' Jiaorui said. 'Why don't you tell me something about your past.'

'What past?'

Jiaorui's leg swept out, almost spilling the tea in his hand. 'Faker! I already know all about it.'

'If you know, why ask? Wouldn't it be better if you told me something about your past?'

'My past?' She leaned her head to one side and rubbed her cheek on her shoulder. After a long moment's silence, she softly said, 'There isn't much to tell.' There was another long silence.

'Well then, please tell,' Zhenbao urged. But Jiaorui fell into thought and said nothing, her eyes fixed straight ahead. 'How did you and Shihong meet?' he asked.

'In a very ordinary way,' she said. 'The student associations held a meeting in London. I was a representative and so was he.'

'Were you at the University of London?'

'My family sent me to London to study, but the real reason was to find a suitable husband. I was quite young and had no wish at all to get married, but I used this as an excuse to escape from home and have a good time. After a few years of having a good time, my reputation wasn't all that good, so I looked around and grabbed this Shihong fellow.'

Zhenbao kicked her chair lightly. 'And you still haven't had enough of the good times?'

'It's not a question of having enough or not. Once you've learned to do something, you can't just put it aside and give it up.'

'Don't forget that you're in China now,' Zhenbao said with a smile.

Jiaorui finished her tea in one swallow, stood, and spat the tea leaves over the railing. 'In China, you have Chinese freedoms: you can spit on the street if you want.'

The doorbell rang again, and Zhenbao guessed that

it was his brother. It was in fact Dubao, and now that he was back, things took a different turn.

Later on, Zhenbao reviewed the whole scene in his mind. Out on the dusky balcony he hadn't been able to see her clearly; he'd only heard her soft voice secretly rustling, tickling his ear like a breath. There in the dark, her heartrending body slipped out of his mind for a moment, and he had a chance to see what else there was to her. She seemed smart and straightforward, but with the emotions of a still-maturing girl – even though she was a wife already. That, for him, was her most appealing feature. There was a danger here, a danger much greater than simple lust. He could not, must not, get serious about her! It would only be looking for trouble. Maybe . . . maybe it was just her body after all. When a man yearns for a woman's body, then starts to care about her mind, he fools himself into believing that he's in love. Only after possessing her body can he forget her soul. This may be the only way to free himself. And why not? Jiaorui had a lot of lovers – one more or one less wouldn't make much difference. He couldn't pretend that Wang Shihong wouldn't care, but then again it wouldn't make things any worse than they already were, for him.

Suddenly, Zhenbao realized that he was digging for reasons to justify sleeping with this woman. He was mortified, and resolved to avoid her from this point on. He would look for another place to live. As soon as he found something, he would move. Zhenbao asked someone to help him get a bed for his brother in the dormitory at the technical school. With only himself to look after, things were easy to arrange. He'd been taking his lunches at a restaurant near the office; now he went out for dinner too. He stayed away until late at night and went straight to bed.

But one night the phone rang for a long time, and no one picked up. Zhenbao had just run out of his room to get it when he thought he heard Jiaorui's door opening. Afraid of running into her in the dark hallway, he beat a retreat. Jiaorui was groping around in the dark, seemingly unable to find the phone, and since Zhenbao was right by the light switch, he turned it on. He was stunned when he saw Wang Jiaorui in the light. She was wearing pajamas made out of a sarong fabric often worn by overseas Chinese in Southeast Asia, and it looked like she had just come from her bath. The design on the fabric was so heavy and dark that he couldn't tell whether it was snakes and dragons, or grasses and trees, the lines and vines all tangled up together, black and gold flecked with orange and green. Night deepened in the house. The dim lamp-lit hallway felt like a train car traveling from one strange place to another. On the train you meet a woman quite by accident – a woman who could be a friend.

Jiaorui lifted the receiver with one hand, the other hand searching along her side to find a little golden peach-stone button and slip it through its loop. She couldn't get it to button properly. Zhenbao didn't see anything, but he was shaken. His heart hung in midair. Jiaorui had turned sideways, and swept her loose, uncombed hair back across her shoulders. Her face was shadowy and golden, like an idol's; her lowered eyelashes cast long shadows that touched her cheek like the fingers of a small hand. She'd been in such a hurry that she'd lost one of her leather slippers. The bare foot rested on the slippered one.

Zhenbao noticed a trace of heat-rash powder on her ankle. Jiaorui hung up the phone. It was a wrong number. She stood there unsteadily, then sank into a chair, the phone still in her hand. Zhenbao put his hand on the doorknob to show that he didn't intend to chat. He nodded. 'How is it that I haven't seen you lately?' he said. 'I thought you'd melted away like candy.' He knew, of course, that it was he who'd been avoiding her, not the other way around, but jumping in before she'd had a chance to speak was a form of self-defense. It was tiresome, no doubt, but when he saw her, he had to flirt. Some women are like that.

'Am I so sweet?' she replied nonchalantly, feeling around for her slipper with her bare foot.

'I don't know,' Zhenbao replied boldly. 'Haven't tasted.'

Jiaorui gave a little laugh. She still couldn't find the slipper, and Zhenbao couldn't stand it anymore. He walked over and leaned down to pick it up for her, but just then her foot slipped in.

Now he was embarrassed. 'Where have your servants gone?' he demanded, for no reason.

'An old hometown neighbor came to visit the majordomo and amah, and the three of them went off to the Cosmo to have some fun.'

'Oh.' Then, with a smile, he said, 'Aren't you afraid of being alone in the house?'

Jiaorui stood up. Her slippers scuffed along as she went toward her room. 'Afraid of what?'

'You're not afraid of me?'

'What?' she said without turning her head. 'I'm not afraid of being alone with a gentleman!'

Now Zhenbao leaned back against the doorknob, his hand behind him, as if he had no intention of leaving. 'I've never pretended to be a gentleman.'

'A real gentleman doesn't need to pretend.' She had opened her door, but then reached back to flick off the hall light. Zhenbao stood in the darkness, thoroughly shaken. In spite of his excitement, she was gone.

Zhenbao tossed and turned all night, telling himself that it wouldn't matter, that Jiaorui and Rose were not the same, that a married woman who did what she liked was the loosest of women, that he didn't owe her anything. But he felt a sense of duty toward himself. When he thought about Rose, he thought of that night in the car in the open fields when his conduct had been so sterling: How could he shrug off the man he'd shown himself to be?

Two weeks passed, and all at once the weather turned warm. Zhenbao went to work in his shirtsleeves, but before long it started to sprinkle and a chill blew in. He went back during his lunch break to get his coat. It had been hanging on the rack in the hall, but now it was gone. He searched and searched for it and eventually he started to worry. He saw that the living-room door had been left ajar. He pushed it open and there was his coat, hooked on the frame of an oil painting: Jiaorui was sitting on the sofa beneath, quietly lighting a cigarette. Surprised, Zhenbao quickly retreated, squeezing himself out of sight. But he couldn't resist taking another peek. Jiaorui, it turned out, wasn't smoking at all. There was an ashtray on the arm of the sofa, and she struck a match, lit the stub of an old cigarette, and watched it burn all the way down. When at last it singed her fingers, she threw the butt aside, lifted her fingers to her mouth and blew on them lightly, a look of utter contentment on her face. The cloisonné ashtray, he realized, was from his room.

Zhenbao was bewildered, and he slipped away like a thief. It seemed incomprehensible at first, and even after thinking it through, he was mystified: Jiaorui, smitten, sitting near his coat and letting the cigarette scent from his clothes waft down over her. As if that weren't enough, she'd lit his used cigarette butts . . . she really was a child, spoiled rotten, someone who'd always gotten whatever she wanted, and now that she'd run into someone with an ounce of resistance, she dreamed only of him. The mind of a child and the beauty of a grown woman: the most tempting of combinations. Zhenbao could no longer resist.

He still ate dinner in a restaurant and arranged to meet several friends there, but the longer he sat in the crowd the more insipid he found the talk, the more detestable the company. He was impatient throughout the meal, and afterward he jumped on a bus to go back to the apartment. Jiaorui was playing the piano: 'Shadow Waltz,' a tune popular at the time. Hands thrust into his pockets, Zhenbao paced the balcony. The lamp on the piano lit up Jiaorui's face; he had never seen her looking so peaceful. Zhenbao hummed along with the piano, but she seemed not to hear; she just kept playing, beginning a new tune. Zhenbao didn't have the courage to sing. Standing in the doorway, he watched Jiaorui for a long time, tears welling up in his eyes, because he and she were really in the same place now, two people together, body and soul. He wished that she'd look up and see his tears, but instead she kept on playing. Zhenbao started to worry. He came over to turn the pages, intending to distract her. She paid no attention. She wasn't even looking at the music, she knew it all by heart and was focusing only on the unhurried flow of it from the tips of her fingers. Suddenly Zhenbao was angry and afraid. It was as if there were no connection between them. He sat down next to her on the piano bench, put his arm around her, and pulled her close. The music stopped abruptly; she tilted her face – all too skillfully. They kissed. Zhenbao's passion mounted. With a deafening crash he pushed her down onto the keyboard. There was a chaotic tempest of sound. Surely this was different from all the other times she'd been kissed.

Jiaorui's bed was too fancy for Zhenbao; he didn't sleep well on the thick bedding. Even though he rose early, he still felt as if he'd overslept. Combing his hair he found a sliver of clipped fingernail, a tiny red crescent moon. She'd scratched him with her long nails; as he was drifting off to sleep, he'd seen her sitting on the bed clipping them. Had there been a moon that night? He hadn't checked, but it must have been a red crescent moon.

After that, he came straight home after work, sitting on the top of a double-decker bus and facing the setting sun, the windowpane a sheet of light as the bus roared toward the sun, toward his happiness, his shameful happiness. How could it not be shameful? His woman ate another man's rice, lived in another man's house, went by another man's name. But feeling that he shouldn't be doing this only made his happiness more perfect.

It was as if he'd fallen from a great height. An object that falls from high above is many times heavier than its original weight. Jiaorui, struck by that startlingly great weight, was knocked dizzy.

'I really love you,' she said. But she was mocking him still, just a little. 'Want to know something? Every day, when I sit here waiting for you to come back, I hear the elevator slowly clanking its way up. When it goes past our floor without stopping, it feels like my own heart's gone up, that it's just hanging in midair. But when the elevator stops before it reaches our floor, it seems like my breath's been cut off.'

'So – there's an elevator in your heart. It looks as though your heart is still an apartment.'

Jiaorui smiled gently, then walked over to the

window and looked out, hands clasped behind her back. After a moment, she said, 'The house that you wanted has been built.'

At first Zhenbao didn't understand; when he did, he was staggered. He'd never been one to fool around with words, but now he tried something new. Taking a pen from the desk, he wrote 'Happy heartwarming! Many congratulations on your new home!' And yet he couldn't really say that he was pleased. The thrill of pleasure had made his whole body sing, but all at once it was quiet. Now there was only a desolate calm; he felt sated and empty at the same time.

When they embraced again, Jiaorui wrapped herself around him, she held him so tightly that she blushed. 'It's the same, isn't it, even if there's no love? If I could be like this with you, without any real feeling of love, you'd certainly lose all respect for me.' She gripped him still more tightly. 'Don't you feel the difference? Don't you?'

'Of course I do.' But actually he couldn't tell. The old Jiaorui had been too good at feigning love.

Never before had she been in love like this. Even she didn't know why she loved Zhenbao so much. She'd watch him closely, her gaze both tender and mocking, mocking him and mocking herself.

He was a man with a future, of course, a top-notch

textile engineer. His working style was special: nose to the grindstone, too busy to lift his head. The foreign boss was constantly calling for him: 'Tong! Tong! Where's Tong?' Zhenbao pushed a lock of hair from his forehead, eyes gleaming behind his glasses, the frames flashing. He liked summer, but even when it wasn't summer he'd be so busy that he'd work up a sweat. The elbows and knees of his Western-style suit were full of creases like laugh lines. Chinese colleagues would complain about the shabby way he looked.

He told Jiaorui how competent he was and how efficient. She praised him, rubbing his hair. 'Oh yes. My little one is really talented. But you know that. If you didn't, where would we be? It's in other ways that you're not so clever. I love you – did you know that? I love you.'

He showed off in front of her, and she showed off in front of him. The only thing she was really good at was leading men on. Like the tumbler who excelled at turning somersaults and turned somersaults for the Virgin Mary, Jiaorui was sincerely pious: she offered up her art to her beloved. She'd provoke a man, and when he responded accordingly, she'd glance over at Zhenbao with a humble smile, as if to say, 'This is what *I* know – and if I didn't, where would we be?' That Timmy Sun of hers was still in a sulk, and yet she found ways to tease him. Zhenbao understood what she was doing; it was tiresome, he thought, but he put up with it because it was just her childishness. Being with Jiaorui was like living with a swarm of teenagers – enough to make you old in no time.

Sometimes they discussed her husband's return. Zhenbao would wear a dark, defeated smile. His eyes and his eyebrows drooped; his whole face hung down in a mess like a mop. The entire relationship was illicit, but he kept using this sinfulness as a spur, pushing himself to love her even more fiercely. Jiaorui didn't understand the full nature of his feeling, but it made her happy to see him suffer. Back when she was a student in England – jumping out of bed, putting on lipstick without even bothering to wash her face, and running out to see her boyfriends – men had of course threatened to kill themselves for her sake. 'I spent the whole night pacing under your window,' they'd say. 'I couldn't sleep.' That meant nothing. But making a man suffer for real – that was something else again.

One day she said, 'I've been thinking about how to tell him when he comes back,' just as if it had already been decided that she would inform Shihong about everything, divorce him, and marry Zhenbao. Zhenbao wasn't brave enough to say anything then. But his dark, defeated smile was not having the desired effect, so later on he said, 'Let's not rush into this blindly. Let me talk to a lawyer friend of mine first – get things clear. You know, if this isn't handled properly, there could be quite a price to pay.' As a businessman, he felt that merely by uttering the word 'lawyer' he'd gotten seriously involved in something – much too seriously. But Jiaorui didn't notice his qualms. She was full of confidence, sure that once the problem on her side was solved, it would all be clear sailing.

Jiaorui often called him at his office. She had no restraint, and it upset him. One day she phoned to say, 'Why don't we go out later and have some fun?'

Zhenbao wanted to know why she was so happy.

'You like me to wear those prim and proper Chinese fashions, don't you? I had a new outfit made, and it came today. I want to wear it someplace.'

'How about a movie?'

He and some colleagues had chipped in together to buy a small car, and Jiaorui liked to go out for a ride. She had a plan that Zhenbao was going to teach her to drive. 'After I've learned I'll buy a car too,' she announced. So Shihong would buy it for her? Her words stuck in Zhenbao's craw; he couldn't quite digest it.

Jiaorui didn't seem all that excited about seeing a movie. 'Okay,' she said, 'if we can take the car.'

'So what are your feet for?' he laughed.

'Chasing you!' And she laughed too. After that, things got busy at the office. Zhenbao had to get off the phone.

But that day another colleague happened to need the car, and Zhenbao was always self-sacrificing, especially when it came to pleasures. He was dropped off at the street corner – from the apartment window Jiaorui saw him stop to buy the evening paper, though she couldn't tell if he was looking at ads for the movies. She rushed out to meet him at the street door. 'If we don't have the car, we can't make it to the 5:15 movie. Let's forget about it.'

Zhenbao looked at her and smiled. 'So do you want to go someplace else? You look great.'

Jiaorui hooked her arm in his. 'Won't it be fun just to walk along the avenue?'

But Zhenbao kept fretting, wanting to know how she felt about this place, then that one. They passed a Western-style restaurant with music. She turned it down. 'The truth is, I'm pretty broke these days!' he said.

'Oh, dear,' she laughed. 'If I'd known that, I'd never have gotten mixed up with you!'

Just then, Zhenbao recognized an old foreign lady that he knew – somebody through whom his family had sent money and packages when he was studying abroad. Mrs Ashe was British but she'd married a Eurasian, which made her self-conscious and as British as British can be. She was tall and stooped and wore an elaborate dress, a foreign-style print that sagged around her frame and made her look like an old beggar. Her hat was a robin's egg blue, mottled with black, and she'd stuck a pearl-headed hatpin and a swallow feather in it. Under the hat was a circle of gray hair, pressed flat like a wig, and her eyes looked as if they were made of pale blue porcelain. Her English came out very softly, her voice breathy and conspiratorial. Zhenbao shook hands with her. 'Are you still living in the same place?' he asked.

'At first we were going to go home this summer, but my husband just can't get away!' Going to England was 'going home' even though her husband's family had lived in China for three generations, and she herself had no living relatives in England.

Zhenbao introduced Jiaorui. 'This is Mrs Shihong Wang. Wang was in Edinburgh also, and Mrs Wang spent many years in London. I'm living at their place now.'

Mrs Ashe was accompanied by her daughter. Zhenbao, of course, had considerable experience with mixed-blood girls. Miss Ashe pursed her red lips but didn't say much. She had dark brown eyes peering out of a pointed, white-peach face. A woman who doesn't yet have her own household, her own portion of worry and duty and joy, will often have that watchful, waiting look. And yet Miss Ashe, young as she was, didn't yearn for domesticity; she wasn't a girl with a heart 'launched like an arrow toward home.' Career girls in the city often have a harried look, and Miss Ashe's eyes were puffy, her face drawn and pale. In China, as elsewhere, the constraints imposed by the traditional moral code were originally constructed for the benefit of women: they made beautiful women even harder to obtain, so their value rose, and ugly women were spared the prospect of never-ending humiliation. Women nowadays don't have this kind of protective buffer, especially not mixed-blood girls, whose status is so entirely undefined. There was a razor edge to Miss Ashe's exhausted peering gaze.

Jiaorui could see at a glance that in going home mother and daughter would be headed straight into the English lower middle class. But they were Zhenbao's friends, and she was eager to make a good impression; also, for some reason, the presence of other females made her feel like a 'proper woman' again. She was a full-status wife. She ought to exude an air of dignified affluence. Zhenbao rarely saw her smiling so serenely, almost like a movie star; suddenly she became a sapphire from whose depths a flickering lamp draws waves of light and shadow. Jiaorui was wearing a cheongsam of dark purple-blue georgette, and a little heart-shaped gold pendant gleamed faintly at her breast, cold and splendid – as if she had no other heart. Zhenbao looked at her, and he was both pleased and suspicious; if there'd been a man around how different things would have been!

Mrs Ashe asked about Mrs Tong, and Zhenbao said, 'My mother's health is fine. She still looks after the whole family.' He turned to Jiaorui. 'My mother often does the cooking, and she's a very good cook. I always say we're very lucky to have a mother like that!' Whenever he praised his widowed mother, he was reminded of the many years of grievous hardship his family had endured, and he couldn't help gnashing his teeth. He smiled, but as the full weight of his ambitions bore down on him, his heart was like a rock.

Mrs Ashe asked about his younger brother and sisters. 'Dubao is a good kid, he's in technical school now, and later on our factory might send him to England to study.' Even the two sisters were praised – the whole family was ideal – until Mrs Ashe had to exclaim, 'You really are something! I've always said that your mother must be very proud of you!' Zhenbao was suitably modest. He asked how things were going for everyone in the Ashe family.

Seeing the newspaper rolled up in his hand, Mrs Ashe inquired if there was any news this evening. Zhenbao handed her the paper, but her eyesight was so poor that even when she held it at arm's length she still couldn't make anything out. She asked her daughter to read it for her.

'I was planning to take Mrs Wang to see a movie, but there aren't any good ones,' Zhenbao said. In front of other people his attitude toward Jiaorui was a little stiff – he wanted to show that he was only a family friend – but Miss Ashe's quiet, watchful eyes made him feel he was giving everything away. Zhenbao leaned close to Jiaorui. Very familiarly, he said, 'I'll make it up to you another time, okay?' He looked at her with shining eyes and laughed. Immediately after, he was sorry – as if he'd gotten too excited while talking and sprayed spit in someone's face. He had always taken this Miss Ashe for a keen observer. She was young and she had nothing, not even a personality; she was just waiting for the approach of everything in the world. Already its huge shadow had fallen across her otherwise expressionless features.

Jiaorui was young, and she had all sorts of things, but somehow they didn't count. She seemed scatterbrained, like a child who goes out and picks dozens of violets, one by one, gathers them into a bunch and tosses them all away. Zhenbao had only his future to bank on, a future he'd prepared for all on his own. How could he bear to see it thrown to the wind? Rich young men and women are free to be careless – security is an inheritance for them – but for him it was not so easy! The four of them walked slowly down the same street, Mrs Ashe in the safety and comfort of a room full of flowered wallpaper, while the three young people faced menace on every side – it boomed beneath them like a drum.

It was not yet dark, but the neon lights were shining; in the daylight they looked even more artificial, like costume jewelry. They passed a shop with lamps for sale, innumerable lamps under the neon glow, the whole place blazing with light. Behind the tin grill of a snack shop, a waitress leaned forward to pick up a piece of pastry; her rouge-red cheeks looked good enough to eat. Did old people also see it like that? Walking next to the old woman, Zhenbao couldn't help feeling the brevity of youth. A row of shiny round-head spikes, their heads indented on four sides, marked off a pedestrian crosswalk; beside them the asphalt road looked as dark and soft as rubber. Zhenbao swayed along, letting his body go. He couldn't tell whether it was his own gait that was rubbery or the road underfoot.

Mrs Ashe praised the fabric of Jiaorui's dress. Then

she said, 'I saw a piece like that, last time I was at the Huilou fine goods shop. Dolly turned it down because she thought it was too dark. I still wanted to buy it, but then I thought, well, I don't often have an occasion for wearing such clothes . . .' She didn't seem to feel that what she said was sad, but the others all fell silent, unable to respond. 'So Mr Ashe must be very busy?' Zhenbao finally asked.

'Oh, yes. Otherwise, we'd go home for a visit this summer. But he really can't get away!'

'Some Sunday when I have the car, I'll come and fetch you all and take you to Jiangwan to have some Chinese snacks made by my mother.'

'That would be wonderful! My husband simply dotes on Chinese things!'

She sounded just like a rich foreign visitor; no one would have guessed that her husband was half Chinese.

After saying good-bye to Mrs Ashe and her daughter, Zhenbao remarked to Jiaorui, as if in explanation, 'That Mrs Ashe is a really good person.'

Jiaorui looked at him and smiled. 'I think you are a really good person.'

'Just how am I so very good?' Suddenly his face was right in hers.

'I'll tell you – don't get angry. When a woman sees a man who's good like you, she wants to fix him up with someone else. She doesn't even think of keeping him for herself.'

'So you don't like good men?'

'When a woman likes a good man it's because she thinks she can trap him.'

'Oh-ho! So you're planning to trap me, is that it?'

Jiaorui paused. She gave him a sideways glance and started to smile but she stopped. 'This time, it's the bad girl who's been trapped!'

That sideways glance, those soft words – they were intolerable to him at the moment. Later that evening, stretched out in Jiaorui's bed, he thought about the meeting with Mrs Ashe on the street, about his studies in Edinburgh, when his family had sent him money and packages, and about how it was now time to repay his mother. He wanted to get ahead, move up in the world, and the first step was to rise in his profession. After he'd made it to a suitably high position, he'd contribute something to society – for instance, he could set up an industrial-science school for poor boys, or a model textile factory in his hometown, Jiangwan. Vague as it all was, even now he had a fuzzy intimation of the warm welcome awaiting him – not just from his own mother but from a whole world of mothers, tearful, and with eyes only for him.

Jiaorui was fast asleep, curled up close to him, the

sound of her breathing loud in his ear. Suddenly she seemed a thing apart, and somehow alien. He sat up on the edge of the bed and groped around in the dark until he found a cigarette and lit it. He didn't think Jiaorui had noticed, but in fact she was awake. After a long while she reached out, feeling for his hand. 'Don't worry,' she said softly, 'I'll be good.' She laid his hand on her shoulder.

Her words made him weep, but the tears too were a thing apart, and somehow alien.

Zhenbao didn't answer, letting his hands roam over familiar places. Soon the sun would rise. The city was full of the muffled noise of crowing cocks.

The next day, they spoke again of her husband's return. 'Anyway, he'll be back sometime in the next few days,' Jiaorui said with great certainty.

Zhenbao asked her how she knew, and only then did she tell him that she'd sent Shihong a letter by airmail telling him everything and asking for her freedom. Zhenbao gasped, the sound coming from deep within. He stood up and ran out onto the street. When he looked back at the towering apartment building, with its tall, flowing red-and-gray lines, it looked like a roaring train – incredibly huge and barreling straight down upon him, blocking out sun and moon. The situation was beyond repair. He'd thought that he had it all under control and that he could stop whenever he wanted, but now things had rushed forward on their own, there was no use in even arguing. The worst thing was that he didn't even want to argue – not when he was with her. It was so clear, then, that they loved each other and should go on loving each other. It was only when she wasn't there that he could think up all sorts of reasons against it. Right now, for instance, it struck him as all too likely that he'd been played for a fool in a deeper game with her true love, Timmy Sun. She'd pulled the wool over Zhenbao's eyes by saying that it was because of him that she wanted a divorce, and now if there was a scandal, *his* future would be ruined.

He walked a long way without caring where. At a little restaurant, he had a few drinks and a bite to eat. When he came out, his stomach hurt. He got into a rickshaw, thinking he would visit Dubao in his dormitory, but in the rickshaw his stomach felt worse still. He lost control of himself – the tiniest tremor of pain was more than he could bear – and he panicked. Imagining he had cholera, he told the rickshaw driver to take him to the nearest hospital. Once he'd been admitted, he informed his mother; she rushed to the hospital right away. The next day she came bearing lotus-root powder and grape juice that she'd bought for him. Jiaorui showed up as well. His mother suspected that something was going on between them, and she made sure to scold him in front of Jiaorui.

'Getting sick to your stomach, that's nothing in itself, but I tossed and turned all night, worrying about you – a grown man and you still don't know how to take care of yourself! How on earth am I supposed to look after you all the time? And if I just let you do as you please, I'll be constantly worrying. But if you had a wife, I wouldn't have to. Mrs Wang, please tell him – he'll listen to what his friends say, even if he won't listen to me. Oh, dear! Here I've been waiting so long till you'd finished your schooling and begun your career. Now that you're finally getting somewhere, don't think you can just let go, let everything fall apart! You have to earn the respect you receive. Mrs Wang, please, you tell him for me.'

Jiaorui pretended not to understand Chinese; she just stood there smiling. Zhenbao's thoughts were in fact very similar to his mother's, but when he heard her, he felt that the way she put things was somehow humiliating. He was embarrassed, and found an excuse to send her away.

That left him with Jiaorui. She walked over to the bed and leaned over the white metal railing, her whole body a painful question mark. Zhenbao rolled away impatiently; he couldn't explain and he couldn't escape his mother's logic. Jiaorui closed the curtain, and the sunlight on his pillow turned to cool shadow. She didn't leave, but stayed to nurse him, bringing tea, water, the bedpan. The enamel basin was ice-cold against his skin; her hands were just as cold. When he happened to glance her way, she seized the chance to speak: 'Don't be afraid . . .' He hated her saying that he was afraid; his expression changed, and she stopped. More time passed. 'I have really changed . . .' she said. Again he shifted uncomfortably, to keep her from speaking. 'I won't bring you any trouble, I promise . . .' And then, 'You can't leave me, Zhenbao . . .' Her broken sentences hung in midair like the pendulums of several clocks, each ticking along at a different speed, each following its own logic and reaching its own conclusions, each rising up at a different moment, each hammering its bell at a different time . . . to Zhenbao it seemed that the room was filled with Jiaorui's voice, even though she had long since fallen silent.

Evening came, and with the lamps still unlit she threw herself on him and wept. Even in her humiliation she had strength. Through the blanket and the sheet he could feel the firmness of her arms. But he didn't want her strength; he already had his own.

She threw herself across his waist and legs and she wailed. Her hair, a mess of soft, loose curls, exuded heat like a brazier. She was like a child who's been wronged, who cries so much that she can't stop, doesn't know how to, hoarsely crying on and on, having forgotten why she started to cry in the first place. For Zhenbao it was the same. 'No, no, no . . . Don't go on like this, it won't do . . .' The words required an enormous struggle; he was fighting hard to subdue the surging waves of longing. He spent all his strength in saying 'No, no, no' even though he'd forgotten what it was he meant to refuse.

But finally he found something suitable to say. With great effort, he raised his knees, making her get up. 'Jiaorui,' he said, 'if you love me, then you have to consider my situation. I can't cause my mother pain. Her way of thinking is different from ours, but we have to think about her, since she has only me to depend on. The world would never forgive me. And Shihong is, after all, my friend. Our love can only be love between friends. What happened before is my mistake, and I'm very sorry. But now you've written and told him without letting me know – that's your mistake. Jiaorui, what do you say? When he comes, tell him you were only fooling, that you just wanted him to come back early. He'll believe you – if he wants to.'

Jiaorui lifted a red, swollen face and stared. In a flash, she stood straight up, apparently astonished to find herself in such a state. She took a small mirror out of her purse, glanced into it while tilting her head this way and that, tossed her hair back loosely, wiped her eyes with a handkerchief, blew her nose, and, without looking at him once, walked out.

Zhenbao didn't sleep well that night, and with dawn came new awareness; it seemed as if someone had come during the night and fallen across him, weeping. At first he thought it was a dream, but then he realized that it was Jiaorui: probably she'd been there for a long time now crying. The warmth of the woman's body lay over him like an eiderdown quilt on satin sheets. He luxuriated in the moment, breaking out in a gentle sweat.

When he was fully awake, Jiaorui left without a word. He didn't say anything either. Later he heard that she and Wang Shihong had decided to divorce, but it all seemed very remote. His mother cried in front of him a few times, urging him to marry, and he put it off for a while, then finally agreed. His mother arranged the introductions. 'She's the one then,' he said to himself, when he met Miss Meng Yanli.

They met first in someone's living room. Yanli was standing by a glass door wearing a silk shift with ruddy orange stripes on a gray background. Zhenbao's immediate impression, however, was of a vague, enveloping whiteness. Yanli was tall and slender, like a single straight line; the only hint of a twist or turn came at the tips of her girlish breasts and the jutting bones of her hips. When a breeze stirred, and her dress swept out behind her, it made her look thin and frail. Her face was soft and very pretty, and yet the main effect was of whiteness. Yanli's father had died, and her family's fortunes had gone into decline, but at one time they had been a wealthy merchant family, so the two of them had similar family backgrounds. The young lady was twenty-two years old and would soon be graduating from college. Her college wasn't a very good one, just the best she could get into, but Yanli was a good student in a mediocre place; she studied hard and didn't associate much with her classmates. Her whiteness, like a portable hospital screen, separated her from the bad things in her environment. It also separated her from the things in her books. For ten years now Yanli had gone to school, diligently looking up new words, memorizing charts, copying from the blackboard, but between her and everything else there always seemed to be a white membrane. In middle school, she'd received letters from some boys – the elder brothers of her classmates, for the most part. When her family found out about it, they told her not to get involved with people like that. Yanli had never written back.

Zhenbao planned to marry her in two months, after her graduation. During this time, he took her out to the movies a few times. Yanli rarely spoke or raised her head and always walked a little behind him. She knew very well that according to modern etiquette she should walk in front, let him help her put on her coat and wait on her, but she was uncomfortable exercising her new rights. She hesitated, and this made her seem even slower and more awkward. Zhenbao himself wasn't a natural-born gentleman, but he had worked hard to learn the part: he took the matter seriously and thought Yanli quite remiss in this regard. Fortunately, a shy shrinking manner in a young girl is not too unpleasant.

The engagement was short, and secretly Yanli was very disappointed; she'd always heard that these were the best days of one's life. Even so, she was very happy when the wedding day arrived. That morning, combing her hair while still half asleep, she lifted her arms up, looked in the mirror, and felt a strange sense of invigoration – as if she'd been crammed into a glass test tube and was now pushing her head up to pop the lid off, ready to leap from the present into future. The present was good, but the future would be better. Yanli stretched her arms out of the window of the future, and a vast wind blew through her hair.

The wedding was at Yi Pin Xiang Restaurant, with

the banquet at Dongxing Restaurant. Zhenbao liked to make a good impression, but he was also careful with money – good enough was good enough for him. He rented a new house not far from his office and had his mother come from Jiangwan to live with them. He spent most of his earnings on work-related socializing, so the household budget was very tight. His mother and Yanli got along fairly well, but Zhenbao had many complaints about Yanli and no one to tell them to. Yanli didn't like exercise; even 'the best sort of indoor exercise' had no appeal for her. Zhenbao made a real effort to be a good husband and help her like it, but he didn't feel much physical attraction. At first she'd seemed cute, one undeveloped breast nestling in his hand like a sleeping bird with its own lightly beating heart, its sharp beak pecking at his palm, firm yet without strength – but then his hand had also lost its strength. Later on even this little bit of girlish beauty was gone. Gradually Yanli settled into her new environment, and as she did, she turned into a very dull wife.

Zhenbao started going to prostitutes. Once every three weeks – his life was, in every respect, well regulated. He and some friends would take rooms in a hotel and call in the women; they'd tell their families they'd gone to Suzhou and Hangzhou on business. He wasn't particular about faces, but he liked girls who were dark and a little bit plump. He wanted them fleshy and ashamed, which was his way of taking revenge on Rose and Wang Jiaorui, though he wouldn't let himself view it that way. If such a thing did enter his mind, he immediately reproached himself for desecrating treasured memories. For these two lovers, he reserved a sensitive spot, a sacred corner of his heart. Wang Jiaorui and Rose gradually became so mixed up in his mind that they became one: a naïve, passionate girl who had doted on him, a girl with no brains, or anything to cause him any trouble, though he – with his self-denying logic and steely, superhuman will – had left her.

Yanli had no idea about the prostitutes. She loved him simply because he, among so many others, happened to be her man. She was always saying things like 'Wait and ask Zhenbao about it' or 'Better take an umbrella, Zhenbao said it's going to rain.' Zhenbao was her God, and assuming that role was no problem for him. When Yanli made a mistake, he'd reprimand her in front of other people, and if something escaped his attention, it never failed to escape his mother's. Each time she was scolded in front of the maidservant, Yanli could feel her authority crumbling away beneath her. When her orders weren't carried out, she was again to blame. She hated the disdain in the servants' eyes, and in dealing with them she protected herself by knitting her brows and pouting before she even spokc, her whole face a study in childish chagrin. When she threw a tantrum, she always seemed to be talking back, like a maid or a concubine who has grown used to occupying the bottom rung.

The only time Yanli managed to be mistress of the house – for a few days at least – was when the servants were new, so she liked getting new servants as often as she could. Zhenbao's mother told everyone that her daughter-in-law was useless: 'Poor Zhenbao, working so hard at his job to support the family, but when he comes home he's pestered with all sorts of domestic details. He can't get a moment's peace.' Her words got around to Yanli, and the anger built up in her heart. She grew angrier and angrier, and then she had a child. The delivery was difficult. Yanli felt she'd earned the right to throw a fit. But the child was a girl, and Yanli's mother-in-law had no intention of humoring her. Soon they were irritated with each other all the time. Fortunately, Zhenbao played peacemaker and the embarrassment of a direct confrontation was avoided, but his mother sullenly insisted on moving back to Jiangwan. Zhenbao was very disappointed in his wife: having married her for her tractability, he felt cheated. He was also unhappy with his mother – moving out like that and letting people say he wasn't a good son. He was still busy-busy, but gradually he succumbed to fatigue. Even the smiling wrinkles of his suit looked tired.

When Dubao graduated, Zhenbao, in his role as talent scout, found his brother a job at the factory. But Dubao didn't live up to his potential. Overshadowed by his older brother, he became a loafer, without ambition. He was still single, and quite content to live in a dormitory.

One morning Dubao showed up at Zhenbao's place with a question. The assistant manager of the factory would soon be returning to his home country, and everyone had contributed toward a gift which it was Dubao's job to purchase. Zhenbao advised him to go to a department store and see what sort of silver items they had. The two brothers left the house together and caught the same bus. Zhenbao sat down next to a woman who, without a glance, picked up the child beside her and put him on her lap. Zhenbao didn't pay any attention, but Dubao, sitting across the aisle, gasped in surprise. Lifting himself in his seat, he signaled to Zhenbao with his head. Only then did Zhenbao recognize Jiaorui. She was plumper than before, though certainly not paunchy, as she'd once feared would happen to her. She looked tired, but she was carefully made up, and the pendants of her earrings were gold-colored Burmese Buddha heads. Jiaorui was middle-aged now, and her beauty had turned to plain good looks.

'Mrs Zhu,' said Dubao, smiling, 'it's been a long time!'

Zhenbao remembered hearing that she had remarried – that she was now Mrs Zhu. Jiaorui smiled back. 'Yes, it really has been a long time!' she said.

Zhenbao nodded. 'How have you been?' he asked.

'Just fine, thank you.'

'Have you been in Shanghai all this time?' Dubao asked.

Jiaorui nodded.

'It seems a bit early in the morning for running errands,' he continued.

'It certainly is!' Jiaorui said. She put her hand on the child's shoulder. 'I'm taking him to the dentist. He got a toothache yesterday, kept me up all night with his fussing, and now I've got to take him in early.'

'Which is your stop?' asked Dubao.

'The dentist's office is on the Bund. Are you two going to the office?'

'He is,' said Dubao, 'but I've got to do some shopping.'

'Is everything still the same at the factory?' asked Jiaorui. 'No big changes?'

'Hilton is going back. Now Zhenbao will be the assistant manager.'

'Oh, my! That's wonderful!'

Dubao never talked this much when his older brother was present; Zhenbao could tell that Dubao felt it incumbent on him, under the circumstances, to do the talking. Which meant he must know all about their affair.

Dubao got off at the next stop. Zhenbao was silent for a while. He didn't look at Jiaorui. 'Well, and how are you?' he asked the empty air.

Jiaorui was silent, but after a pause she said, 'Just fine.' The same question and same answer as before, but now they had an entirely different meaning.

'This Mr Zhu – do you love him?'

Jiaorui nodded. When she answered, her words were interrupted by pauses. 'Starting with you . . . I learned . . . how to love . . . to really love. Love is good. Even though I have suffered, I still want to love, and so . . .'

Zhenbao rolled up the square collar of her son's sailor outfit. 'You're very happy,' he said in a low voice.

Jiaorui laughed. 'I had to forge ahead somehow. When I ran into something, well, that was it.'

'What you run into is always a man,' Zhenbao said with a cold smile.

Jiaorui wasn't angry. She tilted her head to one side and thought about it. 'True,' she said. 'When I was young and pretty, I always ran into men. That probably would have happened no matter what I did, once my social life started. But now, there are other things besides men, always other things . . .'

Zhenbao stared at her, unaware that his heart, at that moment, was aching with jealousy.

'And you?' asked Jiaorui. 'How are you?'

Zhenbao wanted to sum up his perfectly happy life in a few simple words, but as he was trying to find them, he looked up and saw his face in the small mirror on the bus driver's right. He knew his face was steady and calm, and yet the vibration of the bus made his face vibrate too, a strange, calm, regular vibration, almost as if his face was being gently massaged. All at once, Zhenbao's face really did begin to quiver; in the mirror he saw tears streaming down . . . he didn't know why. Shouldn't she have been the one to weep? It was all wrong, and yet he couldn't stop. She should be weeping, he should be comforting her. But Jiaorui didn't comfort him. She sat silently for a long time. Then she asked, 'Is this your stop?'

He got off the bus and went to work as usual. It was Saturday, so they had the afternoon off. He went home at half past twelve. He had a small Western-style house with a big, imposing wall out front, but then all the houses in the area, row after row of them, looked exactly the same: gray cement walls, as smooth, shiny, and rectangular as coffins, with flowering oleanders sticking up over the top. The courtyard inside was small, but it counted as a garden. Everything a home should have, his had. Small white clouds floated in the blue sky above, and on the street a flute vendor was playing the flute – a sharp, soft, sinuous, Oriental tune that twisted and turned in the ear like embroidery, like a picture of a dream in a novel, a trail of white mist coming out from under the bed curtain and unfurling all sorts of images, slowly uncoiling like a lazy snake, till finally the drowsiness is just too great, and even the dream falls asleep.

The house was perfectly quiet when Zhenbao walked in. His seven-year-old daughter, Huiying, was still at school; the maidservant had gone to fetch her. Zhenbao didn't want to wait; he told Yanli to go ahead and put the food on the table. He wolfed it down, as if to fill the emptiness in his heart with food.

After eating, he phoned Dubao to ask him how the shopping had gone. Dubao explained that he'd looked at several pieces of silver but none had been suitable. 'I have a pair of silver vases here,' said Zhenbao. 'Someone gave them to us as wedding gifts. Take them to a shop and have them re-engraved. That should take care of it. You can return the money you've collected. It'll be my contribution.' Dubao agreed, and Zhenbao said, 'Perhaps you should come and get them now.' He was anxious to see Dubao and to find out his reaction to seeing Jiaorui that morning. The whole scene had been so nonsensical – and his own response so absurd – that Zhenbao almost wondered if it had really happened.

Dubao came, and Zhenbao casually brought the conversation round to Jiaorui. Dubao tapped his cigarette like a man of experience: 'She's gotten old, really old.' Which apparently meant, for a woman, that she was finished.

Zhenbao reviewed the scene that morning: yes, she had grown old. But even this he envied. He looked at his wife. Eight years of marriage and still no trace of experience. She was hollow and spotless. She always would be.

He told Yanli to wrap up the two silver vases on the mantelpiece and give them to Dubao. She scrambled around to find a chair, removed the cushion, stood on the chair, got some newspaper from the top of the cupboard, went back to the drawer for some string, found a string that was too short, wrapped up the vases and made a complete mess of it, even ripping the paper into pieces. Zhenbao watched the whole thing with growing irritation. All at once he strode over and grabbed the vases from her. He groaned loudly. 'When a person's stupid, everything's a trial!'

Yanli's face flushed with resentment, like a slave

girl's. But then she smiled and laughed, glancing quickly at Dubao to see if he was laughing too, afraid he might not have caught her husband's joke. She stood to one side with her arms folded while Zhenbao wrapped up the silver vases. Her features were strangely clouded, as if a white membrane had been stretched across her face.

Dubao was getting fidgety. At their house friends and relatives often got fidgety. He wanted to leave. Anxious to make up for the faux pas, Yanli rallied. She pressed him warmly to stay – 'If you aren't busy.' She fawned and smiled, her eyes narrowing, her nose wrinkling flirtatiously. She often surprised people with such an unexpected intimacy. If Dubao had been a woman, she would have taken his hand in her own moist palm and held on desperately – imposing herself in a way that was sure to prove distasteful.

Dubao said he really must go. At the door, he ran into the old maidservant bringing Huiying back. Dubao took some gum from his trousers pocket and gave it to the girl. 'Say "Thank you, Uncle,"' Yanli chimed in. Huiying dodged away.

'Ah! So you're embarrassed!' Dubao laughed.

Huiying flipped up her Western-style skirt to hide her face, showing her underwear. 'Now you should be really embarrassed!' Yanli cried out.

Huiying grabbed the gum, flipped the skirt over her face again, and ran away laughing.

Zhenbao sat watching his daughter, with her thin, yellow, prancing hands and feet. Before, this child had not existed. He had summoned her out of thin air.

Zhenbao went upstairs to wash his face; downstairs, Yanli turned on the radio to listen to the news. Zhenbao thought it was a good idea for Yanli to listen to the news – part of a modern woman's education. Perhaps she'd even pick up a phrase or two of Mandarin. He didn't know that Yanli listened to the radio just to hear a human voice.

Zhenbao looked out of the window. The sky was blue and the clouds were white, the oleander was blooming in the courtyard, and the flute was still playing in the street – as sharp and wheedling as the voice of a low-class woman. It wasn't a very good flute. The notes were shrill and hurt his ears.

Here on this lovely spring afternoon, Zhenbao looked around at the world he had made. There was no way to destroy it.

The quiet house was filled with sunlight. Downstairs, a man's confident voice came over the radio, droning on and on.

From the moment Zhenbao got married, he'd been convinced that everyone around him, starting with his mother, should be patting him on the back and offering him encouragement. His mother knew how much he'd sacrificed, but he felt that even those who didn't know all the details owed him respect, owed him a little sympathy in compensation.

As a result, people often did make a point of praising him, though never enough, while Zhenbao devoted himself to doing all sorts of good deeds – things he'd take upon himself, without even being asked. He paid off some debts for Dubao, found him a wife, set him up in a house with his family. His sister was a particular problem, and this made him especially considerate toward unmarried or widowed friends. He got them jobs, money – there was nothing he wouldn't do. He spent a lot of time and effort obtaining a position for his sister at a school in the interior, because he'd heard that the male teachers there were all recent university graduates, every one of them unmarried. But his sister wasn't cut out for hardship; she threw a fit and came running back to Shanghai, not even finishing out her half-year contract. His mother sympathized with her daughter, and criticized Zhenbao for being hasty.

Yanli watched all this from the sidelines. It made her very angry on Zhenbao's behalf, and she complained to others whenever she could. But Yanli rarely saw anyone. Lacking a lively, sociable lady of the house,

Zhenbao felt it was better to take people out, even if it did cost more. He never brought people home. But on those rare occasions when a friend came looking for Zhenbao and found that he wasn't in, Yanli proved an attentive hostess. She'd treat the guest like the closest of friends, freely discussing Zhenbao.

'Zhenbao always gets the short end of the stick – he's so good to people, so sincere, and then he's the one who suffers! Ah – but that's how it is, isn't it, Mr Zhang? Sincerity doesn't get you anywhere nowadays! Even his own sister and brother are ungrateful, not to mention the friends who come around only when they want something – and they're all like that! I've seen it all, and Zhenbao won't change his ways, not one bit, even though he's the one who suffers, each and every time. A good man has no place in our world today! That's how it is, isn't it, Mr Zhang?'

The friend would feel that soon he too would be numbered among the ungrateful, and a chill would creep into his heart. None of Zhenbao's friends liked Yanli, even though she was pretty, quiet, and refined, just the wife for someone else, a perfect backdrop for men busily engaged in vigorous, freewheeling conversation.

Yanli had no women friends of her own, so she had no chance to compare her life with others' and find out how low she'd fallen in her own household. Zhenbao didn't encourage her to interact with other married women because he knew that she wasn't up to it. Placed in an unfamiliar situation, she would just reveal all her weaknesses and encourage gossip. He forgave her for telling people he was unappreciated, because a woman's perspective is always limited. Anyway, she was protecting him; she hated to see him exploited. But when she made similar comments to the old maidservant, Zhenbao's temper got the better of him and he intervened. Then there was the time he heard Yanli complaining to eight-year-old Huiying. He didn't say anything about it, but not long after he sent Huiying off to boarding school. The house grew even quieter.

Yanli began to suffer from constipation. She sat in the bathroom for several hours each day. That was the only place where it was all right to do nothing, say nothing, think nothing. The rest of the time she also did nothing, said nothing, and thought nothing, but she always felt a little uneasy about it. Only in the day-lit bathroom could she settle down and feel rooted. Yanli bent her head and stared at her own snow-white stomach, that stretch of pure gleaming white. Sometimes she stuck it out; sometimes she sucked it in. Her navel also changed its appearance: now it was the eye of a Greek statue – sweet, clean, expressionless – while the next instant it protruded angrily, like the eye of a pagan god, an eye with an evil little smile but adorable even so, with crow's-feet tucked away in the corners.

Zhenbao took Yanli to the doctor and bought her medicine as recommended by newspaper advertisements. Eventually, however, he decided that she wasn't all that concerned – she seemed to want to hang on to her little ailment as if it contributed to her importance. He stopped worrying about it.

One day, he had a business lunch. It was the plum-rain season, and before he'd left the office the rain started. He hailed a rickshaw and went around to his house to fetch his raincoat. On the way he couldn't help remembering that other time, when he was living at Jiaorui's place, when the weather had changed and he'd dashed back in the rain to get his raincoat – that very memorable day. He climbed out of the rickshaw and went in the front door, wrapped in the faint melancholy of his memories, but when he looked he saw that the raincoat wasn't in the closet. His heart thumped hard, and it seemed that events of a decade ago had come to life again. He walked toward the living room, his heart still pounding. He had a strange sense of destiny. His hand was on the doorknob to the living room, he opened it, and Yanli was in the room, along with a tailor who was standing at the end of the sofa. Everything was as usual, and Zhenbao relaxed. Then suddenly he grew tense again. He felt nervous – no doubt because the two other people in the room were nervous too.

'Are you having lunch at home?' Yanli asked.

'No, I came back for my raincoat.'

He looked at the tailor's bundle on the chair, not a trace of moisture on it. It had been raining steadily for at least an hour. The tailor wasn't wearing galoshes. The tailor, when Zhenbao looked at him, seemed a little shaken; he went over to his bundle, pulled out a measuring tape, and started to take Yanli's measurements.

Yanli's hand gestured weakly at Zhenbao. She said, 'Your raincoat's hanging in the kitchen hallway to dry.' She looked as if she meant to push the tailor away and fetch the raincoat herself, but she didn't move. She just stood there while the tailor busied himself about her measurements.

Zhenbao knew that when you touch a woman in front of others after sleeping with her, there's a change in your manner – no mistaking it. He looked at them both with a cold, clear eye. The great white mouth of the rainy day sucked at the window. Outside was nothing but cold disarray; inside everything was sealed off. There was an intense intimacy between those three people enclosed in that single room.

Zhenbao stood high above it all, distantly observing the two inexperienced adulterers. He couldn't understand. How could she choose such a person? Although the tailor was young, his back was already a bit bent. His face was sallow and there were ringworm scars on his scalp. He looked like what he was: a tailor.

Zhenbao went to get his raincoat and put it on, buttoning it up as he walked back to the living room. The tailor was gone.

'Don't know when I'll be back,' Zhenbao said to Yanli. 'Don't wait supper.'

Yanli approached him deferentially and nodded. She seemed to be upset. Her hands wandered around, finding no place to rest but anxious to be doing something. She flipped on the radio. Time for the Mandarin news broadcast again – the voice of another man filled the room. Zhenbao felt there was no need for him to speak, so he turned and left, still buttoning his coat. He had no idea that his coat had so many buttons.

The door to the living room was wide open, and the candid, straightforward man on the radio went on talking confidently: he was always right. Zhenbao thought: 'I've been pretty good to her! I don't love her, but there's nothing I owe her an apology for. I haven't treated her badly. Such a lowly little thing! Probably she knows she's nothing – she wants to find someone even lower than she is if only for comfort's sake. But I've been so good to her, so good!'

Back in the room, Yanli must have felt less than sure of herself: she turned off the radio with a pop. Standing in the entryway, Zhenbao suddenly felt himself choking up. If the man in the radio station, who went on discoursing so fluently, had sensed that his entire audience had all at once shut him off, he would have known what Zhenbao felt – an abrupt blockage, emptiness petrifying the gut. Zhenbao stood on the front steps of his house, facing the rainy street, until a rickshaw came by looking for customers. He got in without bothering to haggle over the fare and was pulled away.

When he came home that evening, the steps were under a foot of water. In the dark and the wet the house looked very different – appropriately enough, he felt. But when he went indoors the hot stifling smell and the line of yellow lamps leading upstairs were as before: the house was still the house; nothing had changed.

At the front door, he removed his shoes and socks, which were soaked through, gave them to the maidservant, and climbed barefoot to the bedroom upstairs. He reached out to flip the switch and saw that the bathroom light was on. When he looked through the half-opened door, the bathroom resembled a narrow hanging scroll in faded yellow-white. The light made

Yanli her own faded yellow color. But never in dynastic history has a painting of a pretty woman taken up such an awkward subject: Yanli was pulling up her pants. She was bent over, about to stand up, and her hair hung down over her face. She had already changed into her flowered white pajama top, which was bunched high up on her chest, half caught under her chin. The pajama pants lay piled around her feet, and her long body wavered over them like a white silkworm. In America, the scene would have made an excellent toilet-paper advertisement, but to Zhenbao's hasty glance it was household filth, like a matted wad of hair on a rainy day – damp and giving off a stagnant, stifling, human scent.

He turned the light on in the bedroom. When Yanli saw that he had returned, she hurriedly asked, 'Did you get your feet wet?'

'I'm going to soak them right away,' Zhenbao responded.

'I'll be right out,' said Yanli. 'I'll tell Amah Yu to go heat some water.'

'She's doing it now.'

Yanli washed her hands and came out, and Amah Yu brought the kettle up. Zhenbao sneezed. 'You've caught a cold!' said Amah Yu. 'Don't you want to close the door?'

Zhenbao closed the door and was alone in the bathroom, the rain still falling hard, clattering on the windowpanes.

There was some sort of potted plant in the bathtub. It had flowers of a tender yellow, and even though it hadn't been out in the rain, it smelled as if it had been. The foot basin was next to the flowerpot, and Zhenbao sat on the edge of the bathtub, bending over to wash his feet, careful not to splash hot water on the flowers. When he bent his head, he caught a whiff of a light, clean scent. He put one leg over the other knee, carefully wiped each toe dry with a towel, and suddenly was overcome with tenderness for himself. He looked at his own flesh, and it was as if someone else was doing the looking – a lover, full of grief because Zhenbao was throwing himself away for nothing.

He shuffled on some slippers and stood at the window looking out. The rain had already tapered off and was gradually coming to a stop. The street was now a river; mirrored in the waves, the streetlamps were like a string of silver arrowheads that shot by, then disappeared. Vehicles thumped past, and behind each one a brilliant white wake unfurled like a peacock's tail, washing across the reflections of the streetlamps. Slowly the white peacock's tail sent out golden stars, then lengthened and faded away. When the vehicle was gone, the white-gold arrowheads returned, shooting across the turbid yellow river and disappearing, shooting by, then gone.

Pressing his hand against the windowpane, Zhenbao was keenly aware of his own hand, his own breath, deeply grieving. He thought of the bottle of brandy in the cabinet. He got it down, poured himself a full glass, and stood looking out the window as he sipped.

Yanli walked up behind him and said, 'That's a good idea – having a glass of brandy to warm your stomach. Otherwise, you'll catch a cold.'

The warm brandy went straight to his head; his eyes grew hard and hot. He turned and looked at her with loathing. He hated that kind of tedious, polite small talk, and what he especially hated was this: that she seemed to be peering at him behind his back, trying to find out how much he knew.

In the following two weeks Yanli kept peering. Apparently she felt that he hadn't changed in any way – that he wasn't suspicious of her – and in time she relaxed and forgot that she'd had something to hide. Zhenbao was befuddled: now it seemed that she didn't have a secret after all. It was like two white doors, tightly shut, flanked by a pair of flickering lamps on a wild plain at night: you pound at them with all your might, absolutely convinced that a murder is taking place inside.

But when the doors open to admit you, there's no such thing. There's not even a building. All you can see, under a few stars, is empty mist and tangled weeds. Now that was truly frightening.

Zhenbao started drinking a lot, openly consorting with women outside the house. It was not at all like before, when he retained some scruples. He came home reeking of drink, or he didn't come home at all, but Yanli always had an excuse, saying that he had a lot of new social obligations for his company that he couldn't refuse. She would never admit that it had anything to do with her. She kept on explaining it away to herself, and when his dissipation gradually got to the point where it couldn't be concealed, she explained it away to others too, smiling slightly, loyally covering up for him. Zhenbao was running wild – almost to the point of bringing prostitutes home with him – but everyone still thought of him as a fine upstanding man, a good man.

For a month it rained constantly. One day, the old maidservant said that Zhenbao's woven silk shirt had shrunk in the wash and needed to be let out. Sitting on the bed with his shoes off, Zhenbao casually remarked, 'Get the tailor to come and fix it.'

'The tailor hasn't come in a long time,' said Amah Yu. 'I wonder if he's gone back to his hometown.'

'Eh?' said Zhenbao, to himself. 'Broken off as easily

as that? Not a bit of real feeling – how dirty, .how petty!'

'Really?' he asked. 'Didn't he come to collect his bill at Dragonboat Festival?'

'His apprentice came,' said Amah Yu.

This Amah Yu had been with them for three years. She folded up some underpants and put them on the edge of the bed, with a light pat. She didn't look at him, but the smile on her gentle old face was meant to be comforting. Zhenbao was filled with anger.

That afternoon he took a woman out for a good time, and purposely went around to his house for some money. The woman sat waiting for him in the pedicab. The sky had just cleared and the water on the street had not yet receded; great clumps of parasol trees shone in the yellow river. Across the street, there was a bluish haze on the green trees around the little red houses; damp yellow smoke came out of the chimneys and flew off at a low angle. Zhenbao returned with the money, smacked his umbrella down, and splashed water all over the girl. She cried out sharply. Zhenbao climbed into the pedicab laughing, full of wet, muddy happiness. He looked at the upstairs window. It must have been Yanli standing there, but what he saw was a tea-tray lace doily, yellowing with age, stuck on the bathroom wall – or maybe it was a little white saucer with a tea-stain splotch in the center. Zhenbao smacked his umbrella into the water again. Break it to bits! Break it to bits!

He couldn't smash up the home he'd made, or his wife, or his daughter, but he could smash himself up, the umbrella whacking the water and the cold, rank mud flying into his face. Again he was filled with tender sorrow for himself, a lover's sorrow, but at the same time a strong-willed self stood opposite the lover, pulling and pushing and fighting with her. He had to be smashed to bits! Smash him to bits!

The pedicab drove through the rippling water, and the water splashed the woman's clothes and her leather shoes and leather handbag. She complained, wanting him to pay for the damage. Zhenbao laughed, threw one arm around her, and kept on splashing the water.

After this, even Yanli ran out of excuses. Zhenbao didn't bring back money for the family, his daughter's tuition went unpaid, and the daily groceries were a problem too. At that point, Yanli became a brave little wife. Suddenly, at the age of nearly thirty, she had grown up. She spoke fluently and compellingly, in tearful, eloquent complaints: 'How ever can we go on like this? It's enough to kill me – the whole family depends on him! At this rate he'll lose his job at the factory . . . It's as if he's gone mad, he doesn't come home, and when he does he hits people and smashes things up. He wasn't like this before! Oh, Mr Liu, can you imagine? Can you tell me what I should do? How am I supposed to cope with this?'

All at once Yanli gained self-confidence. She had social status. She had sympathy. She had friends. One night Zhenbao came back home to find her sitting in the living room talking with Dubao. Of course they were discussing him, and when he appeared, she fell silent. She was dressed all in black, and though the wrinkles on her worried face were visible in the lamplight, she still had an aura of hidden beauty. Zhenbao didn't rush around smashing tables and lamps. He walked in, nodded to Dubao, and said a few words about the weather. He lit a cigarette and sat down casually to discuss current events and the stock market. Finally he said he was tired and would go to bed early. He took his leave of them and headed up the stairs. Yanli simply couldn't understand what was happening – it looked as if she'd been lying. It was all very hard to explain.

After Dubao left, Zhenbao heard Yanli entering the bedroom. Right when she came in the door, he swept the lamp and the hot-water thermos off the little cabinet; they fell to the floor and cracked wide open, smashed to bits. He bent down and picked up the metal base of the lamp, hurling it at her, electrical cord and all. Turning, she fled from the room. Zhenbao felt that she had been completely defeated. He was extremely pleased with himself. He stood there laughing silently, the quiet laughter flowing out of his eyes and spilling over his face like tears.

The old maidservant stood in the doorway gaping, broom and dustpan in hand. Zhenbao turned the light off. She didn't dare enter the room. Zhenbao fell asleep on the bed, slept through to the middle of the night, when mosquito bites woke him. He rose and turned on the light. A pair of Yanli's embroidered slippers were lying in the middle of the floor at cross angles, one a bit ahead, the other a bit behind, like a ghost that was afraid to materialize, walking fearfully, pleadingly toward him. Zhenbao sat on the edge of the bed and stared for a long time. When he lay down again, he sighed. He could feel his old benevolent mood stealing over him bit by bit, wrapping itself around him. Countless worries and duties and mosquitoes buzzed around him, stinging him and sucking at him.

The next day Zhenbao rose and reformed his ways. He made a fresh start and went back to being a good man.

RYŪNOSUKE AKUTAGAWA *Hell Screen*

KINGSLEY AMIS *Dear Illusion*

SAUL BELLOW *Him With His Foot in His Mouth*

DONALD BARTHELME *Some of Us Had Been Threatening Our Friend Colby*

SAMUEL BECKETT *The Expelled*

JORGE LUIS BORGES *The Widow Ching – Pirate*

PAUL BOWLES *The Delicate Prey*

ITALO CALVINO *The Queen's Necklace*

ALBERT CAMUS *The Adulterous Woman*

TRUMAN CAPOTE *Children on Their Birthdays*

ANGELA CARTER *Bluebeard*

RAYMOND CHANDLER *Killer in the Rain*

EILEEN CHANG *Red Rose, White Rose*

G. K. CHESTERTON *The Strange Crime of John Boulnois*

JOSEPH CONRAD *Youth*

ROBERT COOVER *Romance of the Thin Man and the Fat Lady*

ISAK DINESEN *Babette's Feast*

MARGARET DRABBLE *The Gifts of War*

HANS FALLADA *Short Treatise on the Joys of Morphinism*

F. SCOTT FITZGERALD *Babylon Revisited*

IAN FLEMING *The Living Daylights*

E. M. FORSTER *The Machine Stops*

SHIRLEY JACKSON *The Tooth*

HENRY JAMES *The Beast in the Jungle*

M. R. JAMES *Canon Alberic's Scrap-Book*

JAMES JOYCE *Two Gallants*

FRANZ KAFKA *In the Penal Colony*

RUDYARD KIPLING *'They'*

D. H. LAWRENCE *Odour of Chrysanthemums*

PRIMO LEVI *The Magic Paint*

H. P. LOVECRAFT *The Colour Out Of Space*

MALCOLM LOWRY *Lunar Caustic*

CARSON MCCULLERS *Wunderkind*

KATHERINE MANSFIELD *Bliss*

ROBERT MUSIL *Flypaper*

VLADIMIR NABOKOV *Terra Incognita*

R. K. NARAYAN *A Breath of Lucifer*

FRANK O'CONNOR *The Cornet-Player Who Betrayed Ireland*

DOROTHY PARKER *The Sexes*

LUDMILLA PETRUSHEVSKAYA *Through the Wall*

JEAN RHYS *La Grosse Fifi*

SAKI *Filboid Studge, the Story of a Mouse That Helped*

ISAAC BASHEVIS SINGER *The Last Demon*

WILLIAM TREVOR *The Mark-2 Wife*

JOHN UPDIKE *Rich in Russia*

H. G. WELLS *The Door in the Wall*

EUDORA WELTY *Moon Lake*

P. G. WODEHOUSE *The Crime Wave at Blandings*

VIRGINIA WOOLF *The Lady in the Looking-Glass*

STEFAN ZWEIG *Chess*

a little history

Penguin Modern Classics were launched in 1961, and have been shaping the reading habits of generations ever since.

The list began with distinctive grey spines and evocative pictorial covers – a look that, after various incarnations, continues to influence their current design – and with books that are still considered landmark classics today.

Penguin Modern Classics have caused scandal and political change, inspired great films and broken down barriers, whether social, sexual or the boundaries of language itself. They remain the most provocative, groundbreaking, exciting and revolutionary works of the last 100 years (or so).

In 2011, on the fiftieth anniversary of the Modern Classics, we're publishing fifty Mini Modern Classics: the very best short fiction by writers ranging from Beckett to Conrad, Nabokov to Saki, Updike to Wodehouse. Though they don't take long to read, they'll stay with you long after you turn the final page.

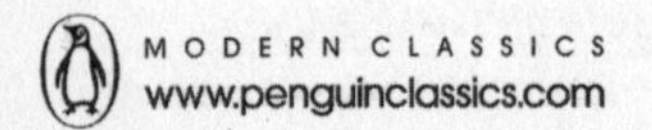